JIM NASIUM

Is a Strikeout King

WRITTEN BY
MARTY MCKNIGHT

ILLUSTRATED BY
CHRIS JONES

CONTENTS

CHAPTER ONE

RIDING THE PINE

We were down by one run, and the bases were loaded with two outs in the final inning. The last chance for my baseball team to win the game. The situation all baseball players picture when they dream of being a home run hero.

I was dreaming. Well, *day*-dreaming, anyway. Sitting at the end of the bench. Riding the pine like usual.

My best friend, Milo Cabrera, sat beside me. Milo was the team's assistant manager and batboy. He usually took his job very seriously. This game was no different as his nose was buried in his clipboard. Just then, he giggled and said, "Ninja Mummy, you're the best."

I looked over Milo's shoulder. Stuck to his clipboard and hidden underneath the stat book was the newest issue of his favorite comic, *Ninja Mummy*.

Okay, maybe he wasn't taking his job *too* seriously.

"Milo!" bellowed Coach Pittman, our gym teacher and baseball coach.

Milo jumped up. "Yes, Coach!"

"We need a pinch hitter. Who do we have left on the bench?"

Uh-oh. I knew the answer to that question. Mostly because *I* was always the answer to that question.

Milo searched his clipboard.

"*It's me*," I said under my breath.

"It's Jim!" Milo reported.

"Grab a bat, Jim!" Coach Pittman barked. "You're up." He waved me over. Coach had his red Bennett City Buffaloes baseball cap pulled low on his head.

We're doomed, I thought. Sure, I was okay with a glove when sent out to right field. But when it came to hitting, my bat was about as useful as a wet spaghetti noodle.

I stood up. My uniform was so clean it almost glowed. I grabbed a helmet and a bat. They shook in my hands.

Coach Pittman's cheeks bulged from the amount of sunflower seeds in his mouth. *Pa-too!* He spit one in the dirt as I stepped out of the dugout.

I pulled the helmet onto my head. It was too big and rattled around.

"All right," Coach Pittman said. He rapped his knuckles on my helmet. "All we need to beat the Vultures is a base hit. You can do it, Jim Nasium!"

***

Yeah, you heard him right. The name's Jim Nasium — don't wear it out!

With a name like mine, I should be a sports sensation. You know, a real gym class hero!

The problem is . . . I lack some serious game.

You've heard that old saying, "born with two left feet." Well, I was born with two left feet AND two left arms!

That's a real problem in baseball. Or any sport, for that matter. And I'd know. At this point, I've tried just about every sport on the planet.

The result? Well, let's just say I've warmed some very nice benches in my day.

But this time is going to be different.

This time, I won't be a strikeout king. I'll be a home run hero!

CHAPTER TWO

BATTER UP!

I sure didn't feel like a home run hero as I walked up to the plate.

The bat was heavy in my hands, and my helmet kept slipping down over my eyes. I raised it up and looked out at the pitcher's mound.

Right at the Vultures' sneering pitcher.

"Swing away, Jim!" Coach Pittman called out.

The Vultures pitcher stared down at me from the pitcher's mound. Everything got super quiet. So quiet I could hear Bobby Studwell talking to Milo in our dugout.

"Get ready to mark another K in your book, Cabrera," Bobby said, "cuz Jim Nasium is gonna strike out again."

Yeah. Bobby's my least favorite person on planet Earth.

I lugged the bat onto my shoulder and stood in the batter's box.

The pitcher wound up and fired. I didn't even see the ball until it hit the catcher's mitt. **THWACK!**

"STEE-RIKE!" shouted the umpire.

"Nice fastball!" the catcher shouted to the pitcher.

I didn't see the next fastball, either. Mostly because my helmet fell over my eyes again.

"STRIKE TWO!"

I lifted my helmet.

"Maybe you should keep your helmet where it was," Bobby scoffed from the dugout. "You're probably better with your eyes closed."

"Studwell," Coach Pittman said. "Knock it off."

I took a deep breath.

I gripped my bat. I was determined to show Bobby — show the whole Buffalo *team* — what I could do.

I dug my feet into the batter's box and squatted low. I fixed my eyes on the pitcher. He ground the ball into his glove and leaned forward.

"Hmmm," the Vultures catcher said. "I wonder what pitch he'll throw. Probably . . . I don't know . . . maybe a *fastball*?"

The pitcher kicked his leg high into the air and fired the ball as hard as he could.

My helmet wasn't in the way. I saw the ball coming this time.

It was almost like it was in slow motion. I could see every stitch as the ball turned and twisted toward the strike zone.

The ball scorched across the heart of the plate.

I swung.

WHIFFF!

THWAP!

I spun around in the batter's box like a tornado in a helmet.

"STEE-RIKE THREE! YER OUT!"

When I finally stopped spinning, I was so dizzy I could hardly walk toward the dugout.

"That's game!" I heard the umpire say outside my swirling vortex. "Vultures win!"

"Bring it in, Buffaloes!" Coach Pittman hollered.

The team groaned and grumbled, mostly about me striking out.

Again.

I walked past Bobby Studwell. Because I was so dizzy, I saw three of him. Three sneering Studwells.

One of him is bad enough! I thought.

"Another K for your collection," Bobby joked. "Better mark it in the book, Cabrera."

Milo looked up from his clipboard. "Huh?" he said.

It was hard to blame him for spacing out. *Ninja Mummy* is really good.

CHAPTER THREE

HIT THE BOOKS

The following day, Milo and I saw a giant poster hanging in the school library. The poster showed an image of a mummy dropkicking a ninja in the stomach. *Author Visit!* the poster read. *Buffalo Turned Comic Superstar, Dirk Devlin!*

"I can't believe I get to meet Dirk Devlin," Milo said. He rubbed his hands together like an evil genius about to unleash an evil plan. "I finally get to ask him all about Ninja Mummy and his black cat sidekick, Meow-Fu. About the Order of the Ancient One and the Mystic Mummy Mind-Flex." Milo closed his eyes and posed like Ninja Mummy about to use his mystical powers to fight some undead creature.

Milo's weird like that.

"I've been reading a ton of *Ninja Mummy* lately," Milo continued. "I can't believe Dirk Devlin, the creator, actually went to our school. And I *really* can't believe he's coming back to visit!"

"I know," I said. "How cool is that?"

I'd only read a few issues of *Ninja Mummy,* but there was a display of books below the sign. So I grabbed a few to check out. Milo and I sat down at one of the tables. I cracked open a *Ninja Mummy* book and began to read.

"What's up, Nasium?"

My heart squished into my throat. Bobby Studwell stood by our table. In his hands, he clutched a towering stack of books. At his side, Tommy Strong hung out, like always.

"Oh no!" Milo said. "Bobby, what are you doing in the library?" Milo was pretending to be concerned. "You poor thing! You must be lost. Let me help you find the cafeteria."

TEE-HEE-HEE!

A few kids around us snickered and tried not to laugh too loud. The librarian, a lady named Ms. Schuster, eyed us over her thick glasses.

"I'm not lost, Cabrera," Bobby said. "I just thought I'd bring Nasium some light reading material."

He dropped the stack of books onto the table with a **THUMP!** Dust swirled around my head, and I fought back a cough.

The books had titles like *Baseball for Beginners* and *So Your Kindergartener Wants to Play T-ball.*

I picked one up and read the title aloud. "How to Be a Better Baseball

Player by Ben . . . Schwarmer? Ben Schwarmer?" I said.

"That's you all right!" Bobby said loudly. "Benchwarmer!"

Bobby and Tommy burst out laughing at their own joke. **HA HA HA HA HA!**

Ms. Schuster pressed her finger to her lips.

"Better start studying, Nasium," Bobby said.

Bobby and Tommy hurried off, trying hard to stifle their laughs and failing.

My ears burned red. I checked out my *Ninja Mummy* books and left the library.

CHAPTER FOUR

PRACTICE MAKES . . . PERFECT?

Later that day, the team met at the field for practice.

"Get a chance to read any of those books?" Bobby asked.

I ignored him and tied my shoes.

BREEP!

Coach Pittman blew his whistle. It was, like, his favorite thing in the world to do. "Gather 'round, Buffalo herd!" he shouted. "Our next game is against the Hudson Hawks, who are undefeated this season."

I gulped, grabbed my mitt, and joined the team around home plate. Everyone knew about the Hawks.

Specifically their pitcher, a hulking Hawk named Hugh Masters.

"But this is a new season," Coach Pittman continued. "And we're hungry for victory!"

"Why's that, Coach?" Milo asked. "Is it because we're standing on a plate?" He pointed down at the white home plate at Coach's feet.

HA HA HA HA HA!

The whole team burst into laughter.

Coach Pittman wasn't amused. "Take the field, boys," he said.

We split into two teams and scrimmaged against each other. This time, I started in right field. I was a pretty good outfielder, if I don't mind saying so. I snagged every pop fly hit to me. I even robbed Bobby Studwell of a home run, catching the ball right before it went over the back fence.

"Great grab, Nasium!" Coach Pittman called out.

Bobby stared at me like his eyes were going to shoot lasers. He gripped his bat so hard I thought he'd break it.

Of course it wasn't my fielding I was worried about. It was my hitting! Or lack thereof, really.

My first at-bat, I didn't even try to swing. Maybe I could get on base without getting a hit. And what do you know? It worked! Bobby walked me, and I jogged down to first base.

Then Ricky Howard snuck a base hit up the middle, and I scurried down to second. I rounded the base and tried for third, but the throw from the infield beat me by almost five steps.

Brad Barker waited for me with one hand on his hip and the ball in his glove. It wasn't even close.

"Out at third!" Coach Pittman called as Brad tagged me.

I jogged back to the dugout with my shoulders slumped.

"It's okay, Jim," Milo said, trying to cheer me up. "You know, it takes longer to get from second to third base than anywhere else on the field."

"Milo, that doesn't make sense," I said. "Each base is the same distance apart."

"Sure," Milo said. "But there's also a *short stop* between second and third!"

HA HA HA! UGH . . .

My teammates laughed. I groaned.
That pun was a stinker, even by Milo's
low standards.

The second time I came up to the
plate was even worse. Bobby threw me
a change-up, a meatball right down the
heart of the plate. It looked too delicious.
I had to swing.

WHIFF!

The bat slipped out of my hands
and flew through the sky. It spun
like a helicopter rotor and hit the
old scoreboard by the dugout with a
thunderous **CLANG!**

"Ha!" Bobby said. "Looks like Nasium's bat finally connected with something."

CHAPTER FIVE

DIRK DEVLIN DAY

Dirk Devlin Day had arrived. The whole school squeezed into the library for the author's visit. It was crazy packed. I was sitting on the floor like a sardine between Milo and Jenny Manzini. At least she didn't *smell* like sardines. She smelled like strawberry bubble gum, which I noticed she was not-so-secretly chewing.

"Children." Ms. Schuster raised her hand in a call for silence. "Let's give a *mighty* Buffalo welcome to the remarkable Mr. Dirk Devlin."

The crowd erupted in cheers. Which was kind of weird since the library was supposed to be the quietest place in the school and all. Dirk Devlin leapt out from behind a bookshelf and surprised us.

"Good afternoon, Buffaloes!" he shouted.

Milo teetered like a weathervane on a windy day. "I think I'm gonna faint," he said. He fanned himself with a copy of *Ninja Mummy*.

"I loved being a student at Bennett City Elementary," Dirk began. "It gave me a chance to try a bunch of different things, to see what I was good at. Sports. Band. Choir. Lion-taming. I tried them all! And . . . well, I wasn't always . . . the *best*."

"Sounds familiar," I whispered to Milo.

"Still," Dirk continued, "when I found out how much I loved to write and draw, I got lucky because Ms. Schuster helped me out. Thanks, Ms. Schuster!"

The librarian smiled bashfully and blushed a deep red. I'm pretty sure I even saw her glasses fog over.

For the next fifteen minutes, Dirk told us about how he learned to draw and how he first created *Ninja Mummy* in elementary school. He even showed us old sketches of Ninja Mummy and Meow-Fu that he drew in third grade!

"Does anyone have any questions?" he finished.

Milo waved his hand eagerly in the air.

"What exactly happens when Ninja Mummy uses his Mystic Mummy Mind-flex?" Milo asked.

"It just means he closes his eyes and trusts his guts," Dirk answered.

"That's impossible. I mean, he's a mummy. He has no guts."

TEE HEE HEE HEE.

"Fair enough," Dirk Devlin said. "It's about instincts. Learning to trust them and not overthinking."

"Oh," Milo said. "Bobby Studwell has zero problem with overthinking."

HA HA HA HA HA HA HA!

Bobby Studwell smiled. I'm not sure he got the joke.

After the discussion, Dirk Devlin sat at a table to sign autographs. We all hurried to form a line. Milo was the first to get his stack of books signed.

Milo shoved the stack of books at him. "I'm, like, your biggest fan," he said.

"Clearly," Dirk Devlin said, eyeing up the tower. He patted his shirt pockets. "Uh-oh. I seem to need a pen. Does anyone have one I can borrow?"

Someone in the back of the line shouted, "Here's one!"

A pen rocketed through the air. It was heading straight toward me.

"Heads up!" Milo shouted.

I reached up and snagged the pen out of the air.

"Whoa," Dirk Devlin said. "Nice grab, kid."

"Thanks," I said shyly.

"Jim here is the best right fielder the Bennett City Buffaloes baseball team has ever had!" Milo boasted, clapping me on the shoulder.

Dirk looked impressed.

"Yeah, he's like a spider in the outfield," Milo said.

"Huh?" Dirk's face wrinkled in confusion.

"Because he's always catching flies!"

HA HA HA HA HA!

The kids in line laughed. So did Dirk Devlin. "Good one, kid," he said.

Milo beamed with pride.

"Maybe I'll have to check out a Buffaloes baseball game while I'm in town," Dirk said.

Milo's jaw nearly scraped the library floor. "That'd be awesome!" he said.

Oh boy, I thought. *More like aw-FUL.*

CHAPTER SIX

BATTING CAGE BARRAGE

"If Dirk Devlin's gonna watch you play baseball," Milo said, "you've gotta learn to hit."

SLURP!

Milo took a loud sip of his Atomic Cherry Mega-Slush.

We stood at the Sir Bats-A-Lot Batting Cages. Around us, the action was fierce.

People of all ages were standing in fenced-in cages. Most of them were doing something that I hadn't done all season — hitting balls!

"Here," Milo said. He swung open the door to an empty cage and passed me a bat. "Go get 'em, dude!"

"I'm not so sure about this," I said as I placed a helmet on my head that actually *fit*. The large, metal pitching machine loomed like a tank about to fire. My knees knocked together as I stood facing the machine.

"Just keep your eye on the ball," Milo instructed. He took another loud swallow of Mega-Slush.

When he plunked a token into the machine, it rattled and hummed to life. Milo stood watching.

I stared down the barrel of the pitching machine.

GULP!

The first ball fired from the machine like a cannonball.

WHOOSH!

I didn't even have time to swing!

The second pitch rocketed toward me.

WHIFF . . . CLANG!

The ball hit the cage behind me. I'd missed it terribly.

The next pitch blew by before I'd even lugged my bat back onto my shoulder.

Jim Nasium, The Strikeout King, strikes (out) again!

The pitching machine unleashed seven more balls at me. Seven more chances to swing. Seven more whiffs.

Someone giggled from the cage next to me. I looked over, and a little girl with pigtails sticking out of her helmet was watching.

"Let me show you how it's done," she said. She calmly put a token in the slot and a ball from her machine shot toward her.

CRACK!

She hit it right off the sweet spot of the bat.

"Show-off," I muttered.

The next pitch from my machine sizzled past my face. "Whoa!" I shouted. Milo had fed the machine another token without me realizing it.

"Come on!" Milo bellowed. "Focus, Jim! Keep your head in the game!"

"That's great advice from the guy who sits in the dugout secretly reading comics instead of watching the game!" I said.

"Hey, my bookkeeping is solid," Milo said. "Right down to every K next to your name."

Another ball thunked out of the machine.

WHOOSH!

I swung and missed. Again.

"Milo, this is a bad idea," I said.

Another pitch.

Another swing.

Another miss.

"You can do it!" Milo threw his arms up, and the Atomic Cherry Mega-Slush flipped out of his hand. Thick, red ooze splashed across the electrical box where he'd dropped in the tokens.

ZZZZAAAKKTT!

The machine sparked and fizzed.

"Uh-oh," I said. "That can't be good."

Suddenly, the pitching machine burped and groaned. Balls began shooting out one after the next.

"AHHH!" I screamed.

I jumped from side to side, trying to avoid the barrage of balls. The sound of them hitting the fence behind me was like a tambourine gone wild.

CLANG! CLINK! CA-CLANG!

It's alive! The machine is alive!

I fell to the ground as balls ricocheted everywhere. "Milo, make it stop!" I shouted, covering my helmet with both arms and curling up on top of home plate.

"I can't!" Milo shouted back. "The machine's been slimed!"

I lay like a turtle cowering in its shell until the manic pitching machine *finally* ran out of ammo.

CHAPTER SEVEN

NINJA NIGHTMARE

I was still reeling from my experience with the baseball-spewing batting cage fueled by Mega-Slurp when I got home.

My little sister was in the living room playing with our cat Vinnie. As I walked in, she held up Vinnie's favorite squeeze toy mouse and said, "Go get it, Vinnie!"

She chucked the toy in my direction.

AHHHHHHHH!

I screamed and ducked for cover behind the couch as the toy mouse sailed over my head.

My dad poked his head in from the kitchen. "Everything okay?" he asked.

"Just wonderful," I replied from my safe spot behind the couch.

I trudged up to my bedroom and plopped down on the bed.

I need to get my mind off baseballs and toy mice, I thought, digging into my backpack. I pulled out the *Ninja Mummy* comics and began to read. I soaked up every word and illustration.

The books were action-packed and filled with groan-worthy bad jokes. I could tell right away why Milo loved them.

As I read, I could feel my eyes getting heavy. I laid my head down on my book and closed my eyes . . . .

***

"Quick! They're all around us!"

It was night. Bright lights shone down on me.

And I was surrounded by ninjas in baseball uniforms!

"What's going on?!" I shouted.

"They're about to attack!" someone next to me said.

I turned, and standing there was —

"Ninja Mummy?" I said.

Ninja Mummy nodded. "Fight now," he said. "Talk later. **HI-YA!**"

He kicked one of the baseball ninjas out of the air. Another attacked, and Ninja Mummy spun around and karate-chopped him in the face.

"There are too many," Ninja Mummy said. "I need your help."

"I don't know kung-fu!" I said.

"Use the Mystic Mummy Mind-Flex," he said. A throwing star shaped like a baseball with giant spikes around it sliced between us.

"I don't know how!"

Ninja Mummy's eyes poked out of a gap in his wrappings. He closed them and said, "Watch and learn."

A ninja dressed in samurai catcher's gear leapt at Ninja Mummy. But a well-placed Mummy Wrap Kick stopped him cold.

With one swirling whip of his mummy wrappings, he disarmed a ninja swinging a Louisville Slugger like it was a sword.

And when a ninja attacked wielding a pair of cleats tied together like a set of nunchucks, Ninja Mummy's Ancient Mummy Breath knocked him out.

It wasn't enough, though! More ninjas swarmed me. I had to do something.

Here goes nothing . . .

I closed my eyes and tried to relax.

I couldn't, though. It suddenly felt like I was sliding into home.

***

"AAAAH!"

THUD!

I fell out of bed and hit the floor hard. Sheets tangled around my legs. A hot rug burn stung my forehead, which had skidded along the carpet.

"OUCH."

Soon, my bedroom door creaked open and my mom poked her head in. "Are you all right, Jim?" she asked.

"I'm fine," I grumbled, climbing back into bed.

"Better get some sleep," she said. "You have a big game tomorrow." She closed the door.

I couldn't sleep. I just stared at the ceiling, feeling like a mummy who was quickly unraveling.

CHAPTER EIGHT

TAKING THE FIELD

The sun shone as I reached the Bennett Elementary baseball field the following afternoon. A king-sized crowd — way bigger than most of our games — was seated in the metal bleachers. I found myself searching for Dirk Devlin.

Thankfully, he wasn't there.

The home dugout was filled with my Buffalo teammates. I sat on the bench and laced up my cleats.

"How are you doing, Jim?" Milo asked. I hadn't talked to him since our batting cage blunder.

"Happy to ride the pine today," I said honestly, patting the wooden bench beside me.

"What's with the carpet burn?" he asked, pointing at the mark on my head left after falling on my floor.

"Never mind," I said, adjusting my cap.

Outside the Hawks' dugout, their pitcher was warming up.

Hugh Masters was tall and mean, with hunched shoulders, beady eyes, and a long nose. With each pitch, I swore the ball was gonna tear a hole right through the catcher's mitt.

Hugh Masters? More like Hugh MONGOUS!

I gulped. Hard.

"All right, Buffaloes!" Coach Pittman said. The wad of sunflower seeds in his mouth sat in his cheek like he was chewing on a boulder. "I'm gonna mix things up a bit. Jim Nasium, you're starting in right field." I heard a couple of teammates groan. Mostly Bobby and Tommy.

Coach Pittman held his hand out. "Now, bring it in."

We piled our hands atop one another.

"One . . . two . . . three . . ." chanted Coach Pittman.

"*GO BUFFALOES!*" we shouted in unison.

The team jogged onto the field. Bobby walked out to the mound. I headed toward right field. As I did, I looked over at the bleachers —

— and right at Dirk Devlin.

The famous author waved when he saw me.

My foot caught the edge of first base, and I tripped.

KER-THUNK!

"OOF!"

I slid across the dirt, coming to a stop right at the lip of the infield.

I sprang to my feet and brushed myself off with my glove. *Well,* I thought, *at least I got my uniform dirty.*

From behind home plate, the umpire shouted, **"PLAY BALL!"**

CHAPTER NINE

SPIDER MAN?

The game was a real pitchers' duel. Hugh Masters and Bobby Studwell were pitching machines set to strikeout mode. Only a couple players from either team reached base or got a hit for most of the game. And yeah, you guessed it, none of the hits were courtesy of yours truly.

My first at-bat, I had a batting cage flashback. When Hugh Masters hurled the ball, I screamed and dropped to the dirt.

THUMP!

The crowd got quiet. Nobody said anything as I stood up.

"Uh . . . strike one?" the ump called.

"Sounds about right," I said, stepping back into the batter's box.

Two more pitches, two more strikes.

The second time at bat, I tried the old Don't Swing At All technique. That backfired. Hugh Masters threw three meatballs down the plate and left me standing there holding my bat like I was a statue of a terrible baseball player.

"STEE-RIKE THREE!" said the ump.

I shuffled back to the dugout.

"It's all right!" Milo said, slapping me on the back. "You'll get it next time!"

"Are you even watching the game?" I asked, checking his clipboard for *Ninja Mummy* comics. Sure enough, he had a comic. But his scoring was up to date. There were two big K's next to my name.

Fortunately, my problems at the plate didn't affect me in the field. I snagged everything hit my way, including a deep, high shot by Hugh Masters.

"Got it!" I yelled, waving off the center fielder, Justin Springfield. My back was to the fence. There was nowhere to go.

I jumped up and . . .

FWUMP!

The ball landed perfectly in my mitt.

"Nice catch, Spider!" I heard Dirk Devlin shout from the stands.

Masters glared at me with his beady eyes.

As we went into the bottom of the seventh, the score was 1-0 Hawks. The Buffalo side of the scoreboard was filled with a row of goose eggs.

Masters must have been getting tired, though, because Tommy Strong led off the inning with a single. It was the first hit we'd had in, like, four innings. Next, Justin Springfield struck out swinging.

"Studwell's up, Barker's on deck!" Milo called out. "And Jiiiiiiiiim Nasium's in the hole!"

I kept my fingers crossed that Bobby Studwell would hit the game-winning home run. He didn't. But he *did* get a double, sending Tommy to third.

The next batter was Brad Barker.

Three quick strikes later, he was slumping his way back to the dugout.

"Two outs!" Coach Pittman said. "Go get 'em, Jim!"

The outcome of the whole game rested on my shoulders.

Gulp.

CHAPTER TEN

LAST CHANCE

I walked up to home plate on wobbly knees.

The bat felt like it weighed a ton. I rested it on my shoulder and stepped into the batter's box.

Hugh Masters leaned forward. His beady eyes darted back and forth like a, well, like a *hawk*!

He wasn't afraid of me.

His first pitch was a fastball.

"STEE-RIKE ONE!" the ump shouted.

My bat hadn't budged.

"Find a good pitch and swing away!" Coach Pittman yelled from the dugout.

"You can do it, Jim!" Milo added.

One person, for sure, who didn't think I could do it was Hugh Masters. He effortlessly fired another fastball.

This time, I swung.

THWAP!

The ball popped into the catcher's mitt before I'd even gotten the bat around.

"STEE-RIKE TWO!"

Masters smirked. He knew he had me.

I stepped out of the batter's box. I looked out at the field. Tommy led off of third base. Bobby was at second. The Hawks players crouched down, gloves at the ready.

I was suddenly reminded of my ninja nightmare. I pictured the opposing players attacking me like the baseball uniform-wearing ninjas from my dream.

That's it!

The Mystic Mummy Mind-flex!

If I was going to be a hero, I needed a little help. It was worth a shot.

Besides, what's the worst that could happen? *Another* strike out?

As Hugh Masters wound up, I imagined I was Ninja Mummy. Masters's arm stretched back, the ball in his grip. He released the ball.

I closed my eyes.

Here goes nothing.

I swung as hard as I could.

CRACK!

I did it! I hit the ball!

My eyes popped open, and I stared at the blue sky for my home run ball.

It wasn't there.

"Run!" shouted the whole team in unison from the Buffalo dugout.

Hugh Masters ran forward off the mound. I looked down and saw the ball dribbling along the dirt in front of me.

"Run!" yelled Coach Pittman. "Run!"

I dropped the bat and scurried toward first base. Masters scrambled to scoop up the ball. He turned and threw.

I dove forward, sliding headfirst into the bag just as the throw reached the outstretched glove of the first baseman.

"SAFE!" the umpire called.

My hand was plastered to the base, and a smile was plastered on my face.

Hugh Masters yelled, "Throw home!"

Tommy was rushing toward home. Above me, the first baseman fired the ball to the catcher. Tommy was the tying run —

— and he was about to be tagged out.

Tommy put on the brakes. He skidded to a stop between third and home, caught in a pickle. He dashed back toward third base.

But Tommy's turnaround was lost on Bobby Studwell. Head down, Bobby barreled around third, paying no attention at all to the third base coach waving at him to stop.

SMACK!

Like a thick-headed bowling ball and his henchman bowling pin, Tommy and Bobby ran directly into one another. They both fell back, landing in the dirt.

The Hawks' third baseman waltzed over and tagged Bobby on the chest.

"YER OUT!" the umpire yelled.

The Hawks flew out of the dugout to celebrate their 1-0 victory.

Milo ran over and helped me up off the dirt. "You did it, Jim!"

"But we lost," I countered.

Milo brushed me off. "But the chance we win another game is far better than the chance of you getting another hit!"

"Um . . . thanks?"

As I walked toward the dugout, Coach Pittman said, "Nice bunt, Nasium."

I didn't want to break it to him that I'd been trying to hit a home run.

Dirk Devlin walked up and stood next to Coach Pittman on the field. "Great effort, Buffaloes!" he said.

Dirk tossed a baseball to me. I bobbled but caught it. Then he handed me a pen. "Any chance I could get you to sign that for me, Jim?" he asked.

"Wait," Milo said, bewildered. "*You* want *his* autograph? Like, the autograph of Jim Nasium?"

"Of course," Dirk said. "It's not every day you see someone get a hit using the Mystic Mummy Mind-Flex."

He noticed!

Milo looked like the computer inside his head had malfunctioned. He wavered, first looking at me, then Dirk, me, Dirk, me, Dirk . . .

THUD!

Milo collapsed in a heap on top of home plate. "I want my mummy," he squeaked.

HA HA HA HA HA!

AUTHOR

Marty McKnight is a freelance writer from St. Paul, Minnesota. He once hit a game winning grand slam . . . in his dreams. He has written many chapter books for young readers.

ILLUSTRATOR

Chris Jones is a children's illustrator based in Canada. He has worked as both a graphic designer and an illustrator. His illustrations have appeared in several magazines and educational publications, and he also has numerous graphic novels and children's books to his credit. Chris is inspired by good music, books, long walks, and generous amounts of coffee.

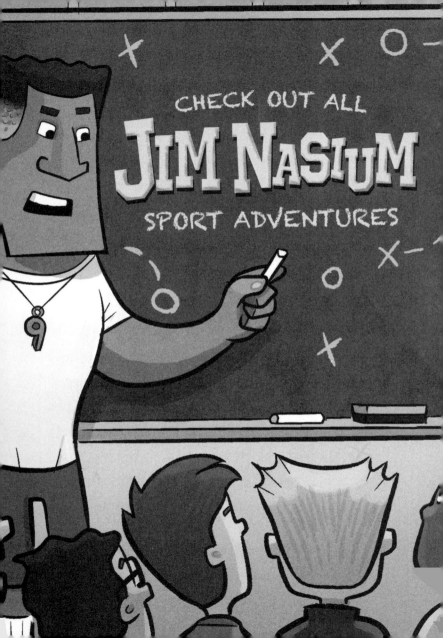

JIM NASIUM Is A Football Fumbler

BY MARTY McKNIGHT & CHRIS JONES

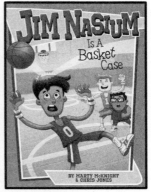

JIM NASIUM Is A Basket Case

BY MARTY McKNIGHT & CHRIS JONES

JIM NASIUM Is A Soccer Goofball

BY MARTY McKNIGHT & CHRIS JONES

JIM NASIUM Is A Hockey Hazard

BY MARTY McKNIGHT & CHRIS JONES

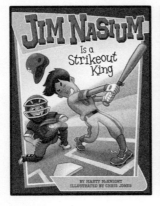

JIM NASIUM Is a Strikeout King

BY MARTY McKNIGHT ILLUSTRATED BY CHRIS JONES

JIM NASIUM Is a Tennis Mismatch

BY MARTY McKNIGHT ILLUSTRATED BY CHRIS JONES